P9-DVO-782

Class Clown

Class Clown

Robert Munsch

ILLUSTRATED BY
MICHAEL MARTCHENKO

NORTH WINDS PRESS

New York Toronto London Auckland Sydney
Mexico City New Delhi Hong Kong Buenos Aires

The illustrations in this book were painted in watercolour on Crescent illustration board.
The type is set in 20 point Gill Sans.

Library and Archives Canada Cataloguing in Publication
Munsch, Robert N., 1945-

Class clown / Robert Munsch ; illustrated by Michael
Martchenko.

ISBN-13: 978-0-439-93593-7
ISBN-10: 0-439-93593-8

I. Martchenko, Michael II. Title.

PS8576.U575C53 2007   jC813'.54   C2006-904965-3

6 5 4 3 2 1   Printed in Canada   07 08 09 10 11

For Leonardo Gomez-Varela
San Antonio, Texas
— *R.M.*

When Leonardo was a baby, his mother laughed all the time. She said, "This baby is *sooooo* funny!"

When Leonardo was one year old, his grandma and grandpa laughed all the time. They said, "This baby is *sooooo* funny!"

4

When Leonardo was three years old, EVERYONE laughed. They said, "This kid is *soooo* funny!"

When Leonardo was in grade one, the kids laughed all the time. They said, "Leonardo is *sooooo* funny! He is our class clown."

But Mrs. Gomez said, "Leonardo, you have to stop! The kids are laughing all the time, and nobody is learning. STOP BEING FUNNY!"

"OK," said Leonardo, and for the first time in his whole life, he stopped being funny.

After one minute, Leonardo felt really strange.

After two minutes, he felt a little bit sick.

After three minutes, he started to chew his fingernails.

After four minutes, he started to rock back and forth in his seat.

After five minutes, he said, "I know that Mrs. Gomez is really tired of me being the class clown, but I just HAVE to do something funny."

So Leonardo looked at the girl sitting next to him and made a funny face.

The girl didn't do anything.

So Leonardo made a really funny face,
and the girl laughed so hard she fell off
her chair and rolled around on the floor.
"Stop!" said Mrs. Gomez.
But the girl kept laughing.

"STOP!" yelled Mrs. Gomez, and finally the girl stopped laughing and got back in her seat.

"What is going on?" said Mrs. Gomez to the girl.

"I was thinking of something very funny," said the girl.

"No thinking in my class," said Mrs. Gomez.

"OK," said the girl. "I will never think again."

"Good!" said Mrs. Gomez.

Leonardo couldn't stop. He said,
"I know that Mrs. Gomez is really, really
tired of me being the class clown, and
I will probably get in big trouble, but
I just HAVE to do something else funny."
So Leonardo leaned over to the boy
next to him and told a funny joke.
The boy didn't do anything.

So Leonardo leaned over again and told a really, really funny joke, and the boy laughed so hard he fell off his chair, rolled around on the floor and kicked over his desk.

"Stop!" said Mrs. Gomez.

The boy kept rolling around on the floor.

"STOP!" yelled Mrs. Gomez. "What is going on?"

"I remembered something very funny," said the boy.

"Well, don't remember anything in my class," said Mrs. Gomez.

"OK," said the boy. "I will never remember anything again."

"Good!" said Mrs. Gomez.

Leonardo was OK till after lunch. Then he said, "I know that Mrs. Gomez is really, really, really tired of me being the class clown, and I will probably get in big trouble, but I just HAVE to do one last funny thing."

So while Mrs. Gomez was writing on the chalkboard, Leonardo drew a funny picture and held it up so everyone could see it.

Nobody laughed.

So Leonardo drew a really, really, REALLY funny picture, held it up, and all the kids in the class laughed so hard they fell off their chairs, rolled around on the floor and knocked over their desks.

"STOP!" yelled Mrs. Gomez. "What's going on?"

"It's Leonardo!" all the kids yelled. "He's being the class clown."

"Leonardo," said Mrs. Gomez, "I have told you to stop being a clown, and now I am getting really, really, REALLY mad!"

"OK!" said Leonardo. "I will never, ever be funny again."

"HA!" said Mrs. Gomez, and she laughed so hard she fell down, rolled around on the floor and kicked over her desk.

She said, "Leonardo, you are *sooooo* funny!"

And that was when Leonardo decided that when he grew up, he was going to be . . .

A CLOWN!